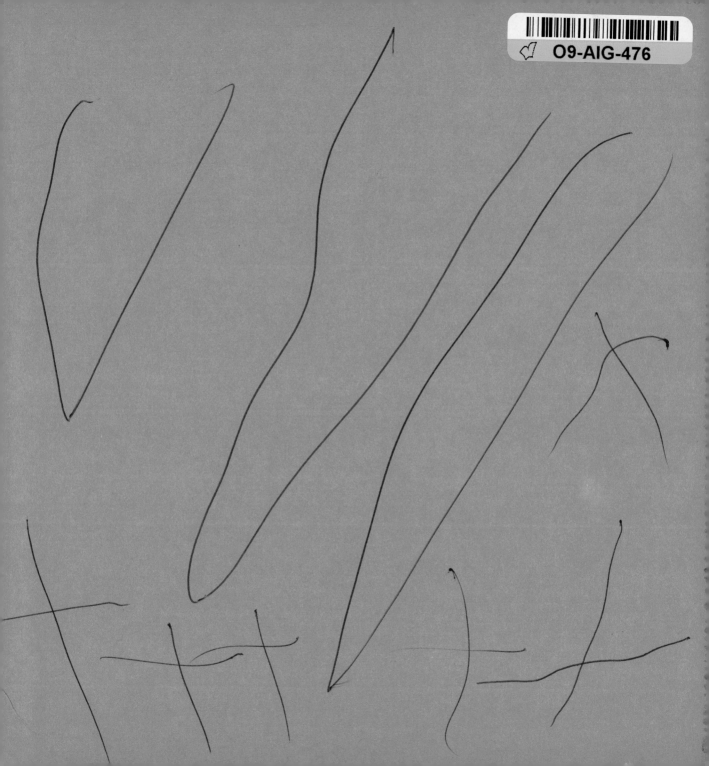

A GOLDEN BOOK • NEW YORK

Golden Books Publishing Company, Inc., New York, New York 10106

Credits:

Super Shape: The New Counselor
Photography by Dennis DiLaura, Ramona Yoh, Patrick Kittel, Robert Guillaume, and Lisa Collins.

Look Look: My Favorite Teacher
Photography by Joe Atlas, Lin Carlson, Patrick Kittel, Barb Miller, Vince Okada, and Lisa Collins.

Look Look: A Day at the Pet Doctor
Photography by Dennis DiLaura, Shirley Ushirogata, Patrick Kittel, Robert Guillaume, and Lisa Collins.

Look Look: My First Pony
Photography by Dennis DiLaura, Mary Hirahara, Patrick Kittel, Steve Alfano, and Lisa Collins.

Barbie Loves Her Sisters:
Story by Mona Muldrow. Photographed by Scott Fugikawa. Photography art directed by Lisa Collins. Styling by Susan Cracraft. Set design by Marty Karabees.

Barbie Loves Weddings:
Story by Jana Pokriefke. Photographed by Dennis DiLaura. Photography art directed by Lisa Collins. Styling by Laura Lynch. Set design by Patrick Kittel.

Barbie Loves Spring:
Story by Elyse Spiewak. Photographed by Willlie Lew. Art directed by Lisa Collins. Styling by Mary Reveles. Set design by Dave Bateman.

Contents

Barbie™
The New Counselor

The New Counselor

By Diane Muldrow

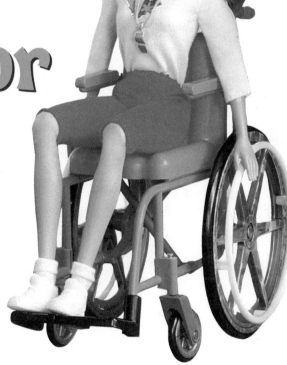

One bright summer morning, Barbie blew her whistle to get her campers' attention.

"Good morning, everyone!" called Barbie. "Before we have breakfast, I have an announcement to make. I'll be away from camp for a few days on a fashion shoot. My friend Becky will take my place as your counselor. She's coming tomorrow so that I can show her the ropes."

Barbie and her hungry campers walked down the hill to the picnic tables, where breakfast was waiting.

"There's more thing I want to tell you about Becky," said Barbie. "She uses a wheelchair. Other than that, she does all the same things as you and me—just a little differently. So let's give her a big welcome tomorrow."

The next afternoon, Barbie and her campers were walking up from the lake when Becky arrived. "I'm so glad you're here!" Barbie told her friend. "Girls, this is Becky!"

"Hi, everybody," said Becky. "We're going to have a great time together!"

Barbie and the girls showed Becky where she would be staying. "Welcome to Cabin Five!" said Barbie. "Stacie, Whitney, and Janet are the campers who stay here."

Meanwhile, the campers were quietly whispering to each other about their new counselor. "I hope Becky is as much fun as Barbie," Whitney told Stacie.

"My friend Lisa uses a wheelchair, and we have lots of fun together," Stacie assured her.

After changing their clothes, Barbie, Becky, and the girls headed to the volleyball court for a game.

Becky tossed the ball up in the air, knocked it way over the net—and scored!

"Wow!" everyone cried. Becky was a good player! The game was a close one, but in the end, Becky's team won.

"That was fun! Everybody made some great shots," said Becky. "Can you show us how to serve?" Stacie asked Becky. As Becky demonstrated, the campers watched her closely.

"Shall we head over to the basketball court next?" Barbie asked Becky and her campers.

"You're in for a real treat now," Barbie said. "Becky is the star player of her basketball team!" Barbie threw Becky a basketball. Becky caught the ball, moved quickly down the court, and tossed it up high. *Swoosh* went the ball—right into the basket!

"I want to be on Becky's team!" shouted Janet.
"Me, too!" cried Stacie.

The campers quickly divided into teams. It was an exciting game! The girls loved watching Becky play. "She's so quick," Stacie said to Barbie. "And she rarely misses a shot!"

When the game was over, Barbie and her campers gathered around Becky. "You're such a good athlete, Becky!" exclaimed Stacie.

"Thanks, Stacie," said Becky.
"What is it like using a wheelchair?" asked Whitney.
"I don't even think about it most of the time," said Becky with a smile.
"In fact, I love doing a lot of the same things as you!"

The campers soon left the basketball court and went back to Cabin Five. "We have free time now, until dinnertime," Stacie told Becky.

"I brought some beads with me," said Becky. "Do you and your friends like to make jewelry?"

Cabin Five was busy until it was time for dinner. Stacie, Whitney, and Janet made necklaces with Becky's pretty beads. "Let's make a friendship bracelet for Becky," Stacie whispered. "We'll give it to her on her last day of camp."

That night after dinner, Barbie, Becky, and all the campers returned to their cabins. In Cabin Five, Becky turned on a flashlight and told Stacie, Whitney, Janet, and Barbie a story about a haunted house. "That was a great ghost story, Becky!" said Stacie.

The next morning, the campers said good-bye to Barbie. "Barbie, we love Becky," they said. "She loves to do all the fun things we do!"

"Becky, are you ready to take over?" asked Barbie.

"You bet I am, Barbie!" Becky said. "And have a good trip!"

"Bye, girls!" Barbie cried as she drove off. "See you next week!"

Barbie™

My Favorite Teacher

My Favorite Teacher

By Diane Muldrow

"Good morning, everyone," said Miss Barbie to her fourth-grade students. "I have an exciting announcement. Yesterday, I talked to Ms. Juniper, the owner of Green Hills Stables, where I board my horse, Nibbles. She's agreed to offer four free riding lessons to the student who reads the most books about horses in one month. So start reading—and good luck!"

"I hope you're planning to enter the contest," Barbie said to Jillian, one of her students later that morning. "You do love horses, don't you?"

"Yes, I do," said Jillian. "But Miss Barbie, you know how much trouble I have reading. I could never win that contest!"

"Don't forget, Jillian," said Miss Barbie, "all the books will be about horses—a subject you like! Why don't you just enter and do your best? Take it one book at a time."

"Okay, I'll try," said Jillian with a smile.

That afternoon, Barbie took her students to the library to choose some books on horses.

"Miss Barbie, I'm starting with this book called *Black Beauty*," said Ashley.

"Here's a book I think I'll try, Miss Barbie," said Jillian.

Barbie looked at Jillian's book. It was called *My Pony*. It had a lot of pictures and not very many words.

"Okay, Jillian," said Barbie. "Go ahead. You can start with this book, but for your next book why don't you try something a little more challenging?"

After dinner, Jillian began to read *My Pony*. It was about a girl
who loved horses, just like Jillian. As she read, Jillian pretended
that she was the girl in the story. Before she knew it, Jillian had
finished the book!

Jillian couldn't wait to get to school the next day to tell Miss
Barbie what she had done. She also couldn't wait to take out
another book!

The next morning, Jillian got to school early and headed straight for the school library. To her surprise, Miss Barbie was sitting at a table preparing her lessons.

"Hi, Miss Barbie!" Jillian said. "Guess what—I've already finished *My Pony*!"

"That's great!" said Barbie. "It's fun to read about things you're interested in, isn't it? Let's get you another book!"

Barbie helped Jillian select a book with more pages and fewer pictures than *My Pony*.

"This book, *A Young Rider*, has harder words," Barbie told Jillian. "But I know you can do it! Remember to sound out the difficult words. And if you don't know what a word means, ask someone or look it up in your dictionary. Just take it one page at a time. Let me know if you need help."

That night, as Jillian opened *A Young Rider*, she remembered Barbie's words: "Just take it one page at a time . . . you can do it!"

The book was about a girl named Jenna and her horse, Stormy. Jenna rode Stormy in a race—and won! As Jillian turned page after page, she could almost smell the crisp hay in Stormy's stall. She could nearly feel the warmth of the sun on Jenna's face as Stormy jumped over fences. Everything seemed so real! Jillian read the book every chance she got. Ten days later, she finished it—and started another book!

CONTEST

Horse Books We Have Re[ad] [this mo]nth

Emily	Kris	Ashley	Gre[g]	[Matt]
14	**4**	**9**	**6**	**8**
Jillian	Dawn	Bonnie	Sta[cy]	[M]ark
4	**2**	**10**	**7**	

WINNER

The weeks flew by. Suddenly, the last day of the contest arrived. Barbie checked the list of horse books that her students had finished.

"Everyone has done a wonderful job," she said. "And the winner is . . . Emily! Emily read fourteen horse books this month, so she will receive four free riding lessons!"

Jillian stared down at her desk. "Emily read fourteen horse books," she thought. "I only read four." Jillian felt so silly. How could she ever have thought she had a chance at winning the contest?

"I decided that we needed another prize—a prize for the most improved reader," Miss Barbie continued. "That prize goes to Jillian! Jillian has come a long way this month. Each book she read was harder than the one before it. We can all learn a lot from Jillian. So, for not giving up, I'm going to take Jillian horseback riding on my very own horse, Nibbles!"

Jillian gasped. "Really?" she cried. "Wow, Miss Barbie, thanks!"

The following Saturday, Barbie took Jillian to Green Hills Stables. "Jillian, this is Nibbles!" said Barbie.

"Hi, Nibbles!" said Jillian happily. "What a nice horse you are!"

Barbie handed Jillian a riding hat. Then she led Nibbles into the ring. "Up you go!" said Barbie as she helped Jillian into the saddle.

"Okay, Jillian!" said Barbie. "Are you ready to go riding?"

"I sure am!" cried Jillian. She could hardly believe she was sitting up so high on a real horse.

Barbie began to lead Nibbles around the ring. "You know, Jillian," she said, "it was a book that got me interested in horses in the first place. I was just about your age, too."

"Really?" asked Jillian, surprised. "What was the book called?"

"*A Young Rider*!" said Barbie with a smile.

"Wow!" exclaimed Jillian. "That was my favorite of all the books I read this month. I was even thinking of reading it again."

"Why not?" asked Barbie. "I read my favorite books over and over."

"But there are so many other books to read!" said Jillian.

"Does this mean you're going to keep reading on your own, even though the contest is over?" asked Barbie.

"Oh, yes, Miss Barbie," said Jillian. "I like going to the public library . . . Whee! This is so much fun!"

After the ride, Barbie helped Jillian out of the saddle. Together they led Nibbles back to her stall.

"I'm very curious about the books you checked out at the library," said Barbie.

"Well," said Jillian, "I thought I should try something besides horse books. So I took out a book about dolphins. It looks really hard, but I'm going to try reading it anyway! And I borrowed another book."

"Really? What is that one called?" asked Barbie.

"It's called *Teacher of the Year*," said Jillian. She looked down shyly. "I took it out because it reminds me of someone I know."

Barbie and Jillian smiled at one another. Then they each gave Nibbles a pat and headed out the stable door.

Barbie™

A Day with the Pet Doctor

A Day with the Pet Doctor

By Katherine Poindexter

Courtney was so excited! Dr. Barbie had invited her to spend the day at her animal clinic. Courtney thought she might like to be a pet doctor, too, one day.

"How did you know you wanted to be a pet doctor?" Courtney asked as Barbie drove them to the clinic.

"I've always loved animals," Barbie said. "When I was in the fourth grade, I guessed how many marbles were in a jar and won a contest. Guess what I won?"

"A book about animals?" Courtney guessed.

"Even better!" Barbie said. "A kitten! I named her Cuddles. She was my very first pet." Barbie grinned. "Maybe that was when it all began."

At Barbie's animal clinic, Courtney was amazed to see all kinds of animals—dogs, cats, birds, even a rabbit! "I guess being a pet doctor is almost like having dozens of pets!" she exclaimed.

"In a way," Dr. Barbie agreed. "But they only stay here until they get well."

Just then, a girl named Megan hurried into the office. She was carrying a big box with a beautiful black cat inside.

"Oh, Dr. Barbie!" she cried. "I'm really worried about Midnight. She's been acting strange and meowing a lot. And her tummy's swollen. Do you think she has a stomachache?"

Dr. Barbie led the two girls into an examining room. Then she gently lifted Midnight out of the box and placed her on the table.

Courtney and Megan watched Dr. Barbie examine the meowing cat.

"Don't worry, Megan," Dr. Barbie said at last with a reassuring smile. "I think I know what's wrong with Midnight."

Courtney and Megan looked at each other. What could be wrong with Midnight that would make Dr. Barbie smile?

"Why don't you leave Midnight here for a few hours?" Dr. Barbie said. "Come back at around noon."

"Okay," Megan said, trying not to worry.

Courtney watched as Barbie examined her next patient. It was a little dog who barked happily and wagged its tail.

"I'm glad to see you again, too, Rascal!" Dr. Barbie said, patting the dog.

"Rascal doesn't look sick to me," Courtney said.

"Not all animals who come to see me are hurt or sick," Dr. Barbie explained. "Just like people, animals need checkups to stay healthy." Barbie gave Rascal his vaccinations—shots to keep him from getting sick.

"I had to get shots from my doctor when I started school," Courtney said.

"Right, just like Rascal," said Dr. Barbie. "See his tags?"

Courtney nodded. "I know what they're for. They show that he's had his shots. And this one has his name and address—in case he ever gets lost."

Barbie checked on several more animals. Then she picked up her medical kit and headed for the door. "Come on, Courtney," she said.

Courtney was disappointed. "Do I have to go home already?" she asked.

Barbie laughed. "Of course not! But not all my patients can come to my office. So we have to go see them."

"You mean some poor animal is so sick it can't even come to the office?" Courtney said, worried.

"Not too sick," Barbie answered. "Just too big!"

When Barbie drove up to a nearby farm, Courtney saw what Barbie meant. "A horse!" Courtney cried.

The farm's owner, Mr. Greene, and his daughter Ashley were leading a horse out of the barn.

"Stardancer cut her nose trying to open her stall," Ashley explained as Dr. Barbie and Courtney approached them.

Barbie examined the horse. "It's not too serious," she said. Then she turned to Stardancer. "But you'll have to be good and keep that cut clean until it heals," she told the horse.

Courtney and Ashley laughed. "But Barbie," Courtney wondered aloud, "how do you get a horse to wash its face?"

"I have a trick," Barbie explained. She and the girls filled a big bucket with clean water. "Now we add something special."

"Medicine?" Courtney guessed.

"No—apples!" Barbie said with a laugh.

"That's Stardancer's favorite treat!" Ashley cried.

Ashley ran to get some apples. Sure enough, Stardancer was more than happy to dunk her nose into the bucket of clean water to bob for them!

"Thanks, Dr. Barbie," Ashley said happily.

On the way back to the office, Dr. Barbie had to hit the brakes. A puppy had dashed into the street right in front of her car!

Dr. Barbie got out to make sure the puppy was all right. Then she spoke to the dog's owner.

"It's very important to keep your dog on a leash," she explained, "especially a puppy who hasn't learned to understand and obey your commands."

The boy promised to do as Dr. Barbie said.

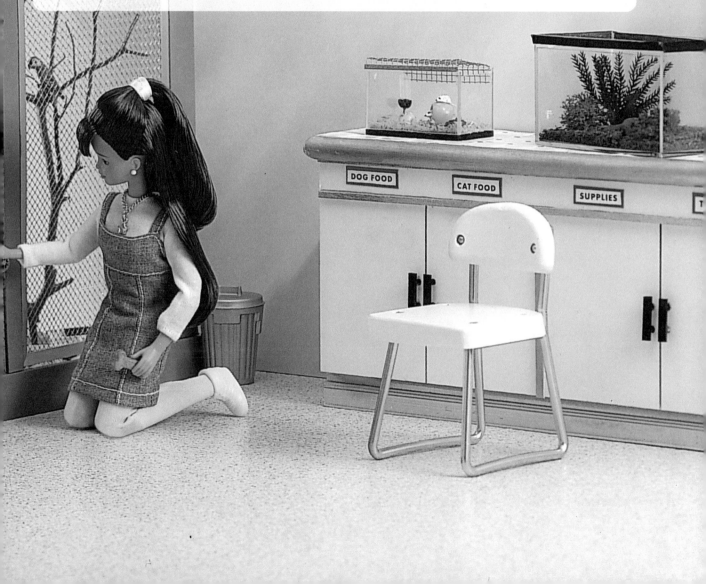

When Barbie and Courtney got back to the animal clinic, Barbie checked on the animals in the kennel. "We keep some animals here overnight," she explained. "Some stay until we're sure they're well enough to go home. Others stay here while their owners are away."

"Like a hotel?" Courtney asked.

"Pretty much!" Barbie answered.

DOG FOOD   CAT FOOD   SUPPLIES   T

EXAM ROOM A

Just as they returned to the waiting room, Megan rushed back into the office. "Oh, Dr. Barbie!" she cried, "I've been so worried about Midnight. Were you able to make her well?"

"She's going to be fine," Dr. Barbie assured her.

"Come on. Let's go see how she's doing. Shhh," Dr. Barbie whispered as she opened the door. "I believe Midnight may have a surprise for you."

Wide-eyed, the girls tiptoed into the room.

"Kittens!" Megan and Courtney exclaimed together.

There was Midnight, resting peacefully with her new kittens snuggled around her.

"How many are there?" Courtney asked quietly.

Megan counted. "One, two, three, four . . . five!" she said. "Aren't they cute! Oh, thank you, Dr. Barbie."

Dr. Barbie smiled.

"The new kittens have to stay with their mother for at least six weeks," Dr. Barbie explained. "You might want to start looking for new homes for them."

"If my mom says it's okay, could I have one?" Courtney asked.

"Sure," said Megan.

"And you didn't even have to guess how many marbles were in a jar like I did!" Dr. Barbie said with a grin.

Barbie™

My First Pony

My First Pony

Written by Mona Miller

"Barbie's here! Barbie's here!" cried Shannon and Amy as they ran toward Barbie. The horses whinnied with excitement.

"Hi, girls!" Barbie greeted them. "How are things here at the Big D Horse Ranch?"

"Great, now that you're here," said Jake as he came out of the stable. Jake was Shannon and Amy's father and owner of the Big D Horse Ranch. Barbie visited the Big D every year to help take care of the horses. "The girls have been talking about your visit for weeks."

"You couldn't have come at a better time," added Jake. "Most of the horses are almost ready to ride, except—"

"Yeah, he's so shy," interrupted Amy.

"And skittish," Shannon said. "He won't let us get near him."

"You must mean *him*!" Barbie exclaimed. At the front of the corral was the most beautiful horse she had ever seen!

Barbie reached over and grabbed a handful of hay from a bale. She held it out over the fence. The horse cocked one of his ears forward and snorted. He didn't move for a long time. Then, slowly, he moved toward Barbie.

"Well, I'll be!" said Jake. "That horse won't usually come to anyone. And he's never taken food from anyone's hand before!"

"Look at the way he nibbles at the feed," Barbie said, laughing. "What's his name?"

"He doesn't have a name yet," Amy replied.

"Then I'm going to give him one," Barbie said. "I'm going to call him Nibbles."

The girls giggled. Nibbles was a perfect name!

Jake suggested that Barbie take care of Nibbles and try to train him since the horse had already taken a liking to her. Barbie gladly agreed!

The very next morning, she got up bright and early to start Nibbles off with a good brushing. But Nibbles backed away from her and whinnied—he didn't like to be brushed.

Barbie started filling a feedbag with barley, oats, and corn. Nibbles's ears perked forward—he liked seeing a full feedbag! Soon he was munching on his hearty breakfast. He didn't notice that Barbie had begun to gently brush him.

"Your mane is so long and pretty, Nibbles," Barbie said soothingly. "And your coat is so soft."

As soon as Nibbles was brushed and fed, Barbie slowly eased a halter over his head. Nibbles shook his head back and forth and snorted—he didn't like halters.

"Now you be good," Barbie said. "I'm just taking you out for some exercise."

Barbie was very firm—and Nibbles must have liked the sound of her voice, because after a while, he finally let her put the halter on him and lead him out to the corral.

Barbie took Nibbles through the paces. She would lead him around the corral, sometimes fast and sometimes slow.

"Clk-clk," she would say to get him to start. "Whoa" meant that she wanted him to stop. And she said "Giddyup" when she wanted him to go faster. They practiced for hours.

At the end of the day, Barbie took Nibbles back to the stable. She fed him again and gave him plenty of water. She cleaned out his hooves with a hoof pick, too. And then she brushed him again and put a nice blanket over his back so that he wouldn't get cold during the night.

"You sure do have a way with horses," Jake told Barbie that night at dinner. "In just a few days, Nibbles has gone from being shy and untameable to being almost rideable."

"I have a long way to go before he'll be ready to ride," Barbie replied. "He still won't let me get anywhere near him with a saddle."

"I'm sure you can do it," said Jake. "And besides, you've got plenty of time to get him used to the idea."

The next morning, Jake and Shannon rounded up the rest of the horses.

"Shannon and I are taking all the horses over to the big prairie on the other side of Angel Canyon to graze," said Jake. "I'm going to leave Amy and Nibbles here with you."

"Are you sure you want to go?" Barbie asked. "The sky looks really dark."

"The weather report said the storm was going to pass right by us," replied Jake. "We'll be fine."

Barbie and Amy waved as Jake, Shannon, and the horses trotted off in a cloud of dust. Nibbles just snorted and stamped his hooves. He didn't like being the only horse left behind.

Barbie started putting Nibbles through his daily paces. "One day, I'm going to ride you," she told him. "I promise you we'll have lots of fun!"

Just then, Amy came racing out of the house.

"Barbie! Barbie!" she yelled. "I just heard on the radio that the big storm is coming back this way!"

"Are you sure?" asked Barbie.

"Yes! The storm turned and there's a flash flood warning for Angel Canyon," Amy said. "We have to warn Dad and Shannon! And they took my horse with them! What are we going to do?"

Barbie knew what she had to do. She ran to the stable and grabbed a saddle. But when she approached Nibbles in the corral, he backed away. She set the saddle on the fence.

"Please, Nibbles," Barbie said, staring into his big brown eyes. "You have to let me ride you—just this once."

Nibbles's ears twitched. And twitched again. Then he calmly stepped forward.

"I knew you would come through!" said Barbie, quickly saddling him. They were off like a shot!

Barbie rode faster than she ever had before! Nibbles was racing at full gallop! His pounding hooves danced over the rocky ground!

They reached Jake and Shannon just in time—right at the entrance to Angel Canyon. The first drops of rain started to fall as everyone headed back to the Big D in a hurry.

"Barbie, you're our hero!" Shannon cheered. Jake agreed to that with a thankful nod.

"I can't take all the credit," Barbie said, throwing her arms around her horse's neck. "Nibbles is the real hero." Then she whispered in his ear, "And you're my friend for life!" Nibbles twitched his ears and whinnied. He liked that!

Barbie™ Loves Her Sisters

Barbie loves her sisters—Skipper, Stacie, and Kelly—and they love her. One of their favorite places to spend the day together is the beach! Barbie and her sisters stay at their cozy beach house that's just a quick walk from the shore.

"Let's put some more sunscreen on," Skipper tells Stacie as they ride the waves on their rafts. "We don't want to get burned."

Baby Kelly likes the ocean, too, but she stays on the shore with her big sister.

A little while later, Stacie and Skipper come up to play on the shore, too. Stacie tosses the Frisbee with Barbie while Skipper relaxes on the beach blanket. She shares a soda with Kelly.

Later, they'll eat a picnic lunch under the umbrella.

After lunch, Kelly digs in the sand with her pail and shovel. It's her favorite thing to do, and sometimes she finds very pretty shells. She gives the pink ones to Barbie.

"The tide is coming in," Skipper says, pushing Stacie on the swing, "And it's getting a bit chilly for rafting."

"Maybe we should do something else," Stacie adds. "Barbie, can we take a bicycle ride?"

Barbie thinks that a ride on the four-seat bicycle is a marvelous idea. Everyone races back to the house to change clothes and get the bicycle.

Barbie, Skipper, and Stacie work together as they pedal down the beach boardwalk. The shore, the blue sky, and the ocean roll by as they go.

"Wheeee!" Kelly squeals from the baby seat. She cannot wait until she is old enough to help her sisters pedal.

After the ride, Barbie decides to work in the flower garden at the house while Skipper and Stacie go for a walk on the beach. Kelly helps Barbie water the flowers.

"You're such a good little gardener," Barbie tells
her. "You must have a green thumb!"
Kelly giggles—her thumbs aren't green.

Storm clouds darken the sky that afternoon, so
Barbie and her sisters go indoors. Skipper reads
Stacie and Kelly a story while Barbie serves cookies
and fresh juice.

"The sound of rain at the beach is so relaxing,"
Barbie says as she sets up a board game to play.
"I wish we could stay here for a whole week."
    Her sisters agree.

Barbie and her sisters return home with lots of memories and pictures from their time at the beach. Skipper, Stacie, and Kelly cannot wait to go back again.

You're
the best sister
Ever!
Love, Skipper
Stacie
and Kelly ♥ ♥

Barbie promises them another trip soon. She
enjoys being with her sisters because she loves
them so much. And they love her—because Barbie
is the best big sister ever!

Barbie loves weddings, especially when the bride-to-be is one of her best friends! Jill asks Barbie to be her maid of honor.

Barbie helps Jill prepare for the big day. First, they make a list of the things that Jill will need to get ready.

Jill and Ben must pick a wedding date. Then, they have to decide where the ceremony will take place. Jill wants it to be outside.

Barbie knows the perfect spot—a lovely garden where the flowers will be in full bloom just in time for the wedding.

Next, Barbie and the bride go shopping for a wedding dress. Jill picks a beautiful full-length gown. She adds a long, lacy veil to complete the outfit.

Barbie decides that she will wear a pink dress and shoes that match. She also finds a cute little dress for Kelly, who will be the flower girl.

A week before Jill's wedding, Barbie invites all their friends to a bridal shower. The party is a secret so everyone has to stay quiet until the bride-to-be arrives.

"Surprise!" they all shout when Jill enters the room.

The big day quickly arrives. Even though Jill is very excited, she tells Barbie that she is also a little nervous.

"Don't worry," Barbie assures her. "You'll be a wonderful bride!"

Everything looks beautiful at the wedding—especially the bride! The groom and his best man, Ken, look handsome and very elegant in their tuxedos.

Barbie smiles happily when the bride and groom say "I do."

Barbie and the guests gather to watch as the newly married couple runs to the horse-drawn carriage that will take them to the reception. The guests all agree that the wedding was gorgeous!

Barbie loves joyful, happy times with special friends, and that's why Barbie loves weddings!

Barbie loves spring. It's such a wonderful time of year!
The shining sun feels warm, and the cool breeze blows her hair.

In the spring, Barbie loves to spend her time outside taking long walks and bicycle rides through the park.

Barbie takes a deep breath. The fresh-cut grass in the park smells great!

There are pretty colors everywhere! Barbie can't believe
her eyes. The sky is filled with butterflies and flying kites.
Pinks, oranges, greens, and blues flutter in the wind.

Barbie gets on her bicycle and pedals down the path.
As she rides along, Barbie sees many people enjoying
the beautiful spring day. They are having such a good time.

Barbie finds a field filled with blooming wildflowers. She takes off her shoes and feels the beautiful flowers tickling her toes.

Barbie picks some wildflowers—but just a few—for her friends.

Barbie joins her friends for a picnic. The food tastes so yummy. Barbie tosses leftover bread crumbs to the quacking ducks. They swim all around the pond to catch the food.

Barbie loves spring because it's the perfect season for everyone to be outdoors!

RPBCGOO